Travis and the Better Mousetrap

BY **Deborah Dennard**

ILLUSTRATED BY
Theresa Burns

COBBLEHILL BOOKS · DUTTON/NEW YORK

Text copyright © 1996 by Deborah Dennard
Illustrations copyright © 1996 by Theresa Burns
Library of Congress Cataloging-in-Publication Data
Dennard, Deborah.   Travis and the better mousetrap /
Deborah Dennard ; illustrated by Theresa Burns.   p.   cm.
Summary: Travis' trap captures not only a Better Mouse, but the Groundhog,
the Easter Bunny, a Thanksgiving turkey, and one of Santa's reindeer as well.
ISBN 0-525-65178-0
[1. Mice—Fiction.   2. Inventions—Fiction.]   I. Burns, Theresa, ill.
II. Title.   PZ7.D4249Tr 1996 [E]—dc20   94–16642   CIP   AC
Published in the United States by Cobblehill Books, an affiliate
of Dutton Children's Books, a division of Penguin Books USA Inc.,
375 Hudson Street, New York, New York 10014
Designed by Kathleen Westray   Printed in Hong Kong   First Edition
10   9   8   7   6   5   4   3   2   1

For Travis, Cole, Alice, and Zachary.
D.D.

To Aunt Lou.
T.B.

"OOOOHHH!" screamed Aunt Millie. "There's that mouse again. I wish someone would build a better mousetrap!"

At Aunt Millie's words, a light turned on inside Travis' head. Travis would do just as his aunt wished. He would build a better mousetrap.

After all, Travis knew that someday he would be an inventor, a scientist, or maybe an engineer. Who else but Travis Jay MacArthur could build a better mousetrap?

He ran to his room. Digging in his closet, he found his tool kit, construction set, notepad, calculator, and measuring tape. From the basement he collected bits and pieces of wood and wire, string and plastic, tube and tape.

Back in his room, Travis set to work.

He hammered and he measured. He tinkered and he fixed. He wired and he balanced. And finally, on the side of his invention, he printed the name: T.J.M. Better Mousetrap.

"Travis, what are you doing?" called Aunt Millie. Aunt Millie was always asking questions like that.

"Nothing, Aunt Millie. Just building a surprise," Travis answered.

"That's nice, dear."

It was time for Travis to test his Better Mousetrap. He carefully placed batteries in the control and pushed the "On" button.

The Better Mousetrap made a clatter and a jangle, a gurgle and a bump, a shiver and a beep.

Suddenly, right before Travis' eyes stood a mouse!
"My, my. How did I get here?" asked the mouse.
"Ah, never mind. Just tell me your name, little boy."
Travis couldn't believe his eyes or his ears. The
mouse stood on two legs and was nearly as tall as
Travis. On his nose he wore spectacles and around
his neck was a polka-dot bow tie.

"I'm Travis Jay MacArthur, inventor of the T.J.M. Better Mousetrap. And I just caught you!" Travis exclaimed in delight.

He paused. "But you're not the mouse that scares my Aunt Millie."

"Oh, no. No, no indeed. I'm no ordinary mouse. I'm the Better Mouse. If you wanted to catch an ordinary mouse, you should have built an ordinary mousetrap. No, my boy, you built a Better Mousetrap, so you caught a Better Mouse."

"Wow! This is great!" Travis said.

"Travis, who are you talking to?" Aunt Millie called.

"Oh, uh, nobody, Aunt Millie. I'm just reading a book. Yea, reading a book out loud."

"That's nice, dear."

"Look, Mr. Mouse . . ."

"Mr. Better Mouse, if you please."

"I like you, I really do, but you can't stay. My Aunt Millie is scared of ordinary mice. If she sees a mouse as big as you, she'll have a fit."

The Better Mouse looked hard at Travis. "Well, that's easy for you to say. But now that you've caught me, how do you plan to get rid of me?" he asked.

"Can't you go back the way you came?" Travis asked.

The Better Mouse scratched his head for a moment. "Maybe and maybe not. Yes, yes, with a few adjustments, it just might be possible. All right, boy. Let's have a look at that machine of yours."

So, with Travis watching, the Better Mouse set to work. Soon the Better Mousetrap made a clatter and a jangle, a gurgle and a bump, a shiver and a beep, and there before Travis and the Better Mouse stood a groundhog!

The Better Mousetrap had caught the Groundhog and it wasn't even Groundhog Day!

Fortunately, the Groundhog was just a normal-sized one. He wrinkled his nose, turned and saw his shadow from the light of the desk lamp.

"That means six more weeks of winter," said the Better Mouse, as the Groundhog squeaked and ran under Travis' bed.

"Travis, what are you doing?" Aunt Millie was coming up the stairs.

"Quick, get in the closet, both of you!" He pushed them in. And just in time, because the door opened and there stood Aunt Millie.

"Travis, what are you doing? I thought I heard funny noises up here."

Travis leaned against the closet door. "Oh,
gee, Aunt Millie. I was just pretending—ahh—
pretending to be an astronaut."

"Well, have fun, dear." And she left.

The Better Mouse and the Groundhog were out of the closet the moment Aunt Millie was gone.

"That was a close call, old boy. Let's get back to work on this contraption of yours," said the Better Mouse.

As the Groundhog peered out from under Travis' bed, the Better Mouse set to work again. "Maybe this will do it," he said.

Soon the T.J.M. Better Mousetrap made a clatter and a jangle, a gurgle and a bump, a shiver and a beep. Travis closed his eyes, crossed his fingers, and took a peek.

The Better Mouse was still there. The Groundhog was still there. And so was—a rabbit, a rabbit holding a large blue and green basket filled with eggs and candy.

"Oh, no, Better Mouse!" cried Travis. "You've trapped the Easter Bunny."

The Easter Bunny said nothing, just hopped around the room, hiding a colored egg here and a piece of candy there.

Travis and the Better Mouse set to work on the machine once again. Soon it made a clatter and a jangle, a gurgle and a bump, a shiver and a beep. And there before their eyes appeared—a turkey. "Gobble, gobble," he cried. "Gobble, gobble."

"Mouse," Travis said in a low voice, pointing his finger at the new visitor. "Mouse, that is the Thanksgiving Turkey!"

"Well, these are delicate matters. And after all, *you* built this machine, I didn't." Before the Better Mouse could finish speaking, Travis heard footsteps.

Aunt Millie! In a hustle and a flash, Travis rushed the Better Mouse, the Groundhog, the Easter Bunny, and the Thanksgiving Turkey into the closet. As he closed the door (a very difficult thing to do), the Better Mouse said, "Tell her you're hungry and bring us some food. The crowd in here won't cooperate on empty stomachs."

The door opened. "Travis, are you all right? What are you doing?" Aunt Millie looked around curiously, too curiously.

"Who, who me?" Travis stammered. "Oh, I was just coming for a snack."

"All right, but no sweets. It's too close to dinnertime. How about an apple?" Aunt Millie asked.

"Yes, yes, an apple, and maybe some sunflower seeds and a carrot?"

Aunt Millie looked closely at him. "Travis, are you sure you're all right?"

Soon Travis was back in his room, delivering seeds, apple, and carrot to the hungry group. He turned to the Better Mouse. "We've got to do something. We've got to send you all back."

Looking thoughtfully at the machine, the Better Mouse nodded in agreement. "Yes, yes I know, and I think I have the problem all worked out. Let me try again."

The Better Mouse began turning knobs and flipping switches on the T.J.M. Better Mousetrap. "Okay, it ought to work this time. Let's give it another try."

Soon the Better Mousetrap made a clatter and a jangle, a gurgle and a bump, a shiver and a beep. And there stood a reindeer wearing tiny silver bells and green holly on his harness and silver tinsel in his antlers. It was one of Santa's reindeer!

The Reindeer joined the Groundhog, the Easter Bunny, and the Thanksgiving Turkey all sitting on Travis' bed. The Better Mouse threw his hands up in the air, and sat down next to the others.

"That's it! I've done my best! I give up!" He crossed his legs, put his arms on his hips, and looked questioningly at Travis. "Well, little boy, how do *you* plan to get rid of us?"

Travis walked around his machine, and paced back and forth in front of the creatures crowded on his bed. Then he nodded.

"Well, Mr. Better Mouse, I've had enough of your little game. I think I know how to get you to leave. You can just meet my Aunt Millie."

With that, Travis turned his back on the Better
Mouse, opened the door, and called as loudly as he
could, "Aunt Millie! Come quick!"

"Oh, no. Oh, no!" cried the Better Mouse.
"You can't mean it. You can't!"

Travis could hear the creatures moving around,
bumping into one another, but he refused to turn
and look at them.

"Travis, Travis, is something the matter?" Aunt Millie was calling. "Travis, what's going on?"

Aunt Millie was in the doorway. Travis heard the T.J.M. Better Mousetrap make a clatter and a jangle, a gurgle and a bump, a shiver and a beep.

"Aunt Millie," said Travis. "The mouse. I think I saw that mouse that scared you—he's right there!"

He turned and pointed to the Better Mouse, but no one was there. No Better Mouse, no Groundhog, no Easter Bunny, Turkey or Reindeer.

Aunt Millie looked and looked. She peered and searched. But try as she did, she saw nothing.

"Travis, I don't see any mouse."

"I didn't think you would, Aunt Millie."

Travis grinned as Aunt Millie left his room.
"I did it!" he exclaimed. "I've just built a
Better Mousetrap, and it *really* works!"